TRUCKER

AND TRAIN

BY Hannah Stark

ILLUSTRATED BY Bob Kolar

CLARION BOOKS HOUGHTON MIFFLIN HARCOURT Boston New York

Trucker loved to rule the road.

He loved the sound of his engine.
He loved the size of his tires.
And most of all, Trucker loved his mighty horn.

HONNNNNNNNNNNNNNNK!

Trucker blasted as he rushed through the city.

The mopeds swayed and gasped.

The cars rattled and gulped.

The pick-ups sputtered but followed in awe.

Trucker was bigger and stronger and
tougher than anyone else on the road.

One day, Trucker went hauling far from the city.

UP, UP, UP he trucked, over the mountains and through the clouds.

Trucker beamed at the sight of the valley below.
He'd never seen such open land and such endless roads.

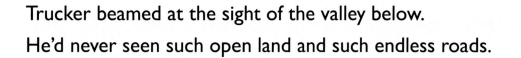

He cruised down the mountain,
letting the breeze cool his hot engine.

WOOOOOOOOOOOOOOO! WOOOOOOOOOOOOOOO!

On the horizon, Trucker spotted a long, strong freight zipping along a track.
"WHO IS THAT?" Trucker revved. He shifted into high gear and raced up
alongside . . . Train!

HONNNNNNK! Trucker blasted at the mopeds.
HONNNNNNK! he blared at the cars.

Trucker gawked at the **2** . . . **4** . . . **6** . . . **8** . . . **10** cars pulled by Train's big black engine.

WOOOOOOOOOOOOOOOO! WOOOOOOOOOOOOOOOO!

Tic-a-tic-a clack. Tic-a-tic-a clack.
Tic-a-tic-a clack. Tic-a-tic-a clack.

The mopeds were smitten.

The cars were captivated.

The pick-ups fell starstruck.

HONNNNN—

But Trucker's tough horn was nothing
next to Train's engine and whistle.

Trucker fumed.
His hubcaps blurred.
He revved his engine with all his might
and proudly pulled ahead of Train.

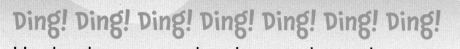

Ding! Ding! Ding! Ding! Ding! Ding! Ding!

Up ahead, two gates closed across the road.

Everyone slowed to a stop.

"Why," Trucker revved, "are WE the ones stopping?"

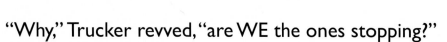

HONNNNNNNNNNK!

The mopeds shook. The cars shuddered. The pick-ups glared.

But no one moved for Trucker. HONNNNNK! HONNNNNK!

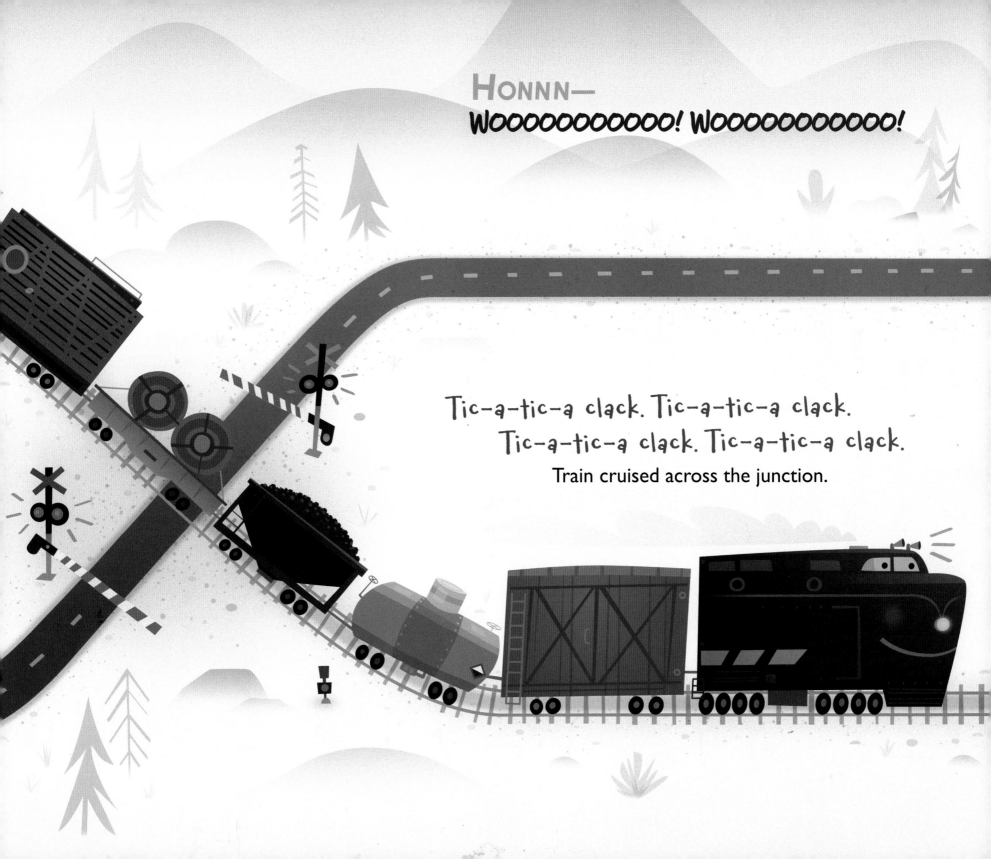

HONNN—
WOOOOOOOOOOO! WOOOOOOOOOOO!

Tic-a-tic-a clack. Tic-a-tic-a clack.
Tic-a-tic-a clack. Tic-a-tic-a clack.
Train cruised across the junction.

The mopeds gleamed.

The cars *wowed.*

The pick-ups swooned!

Everyone was fascinated.

Everyone except Trucker.

Why, Trucker wondered, *don't they ever gleam at me?*

Ding! Ding! Ding! Ding! Ding!

Driving on, Trucker saw Train's track head into a station.
He was happy to see the road bend up into the mountains.

UP, UP, UP Trucker hauled
as the mopeds zipped past,
the cars whizzed by,
and the pick-ups hurried on without even a glance.

HONK! HONK! Trucker tried to greet them.
REV! REV! Trucker tried to play.

But no one seemed to notice.

No one seemed to care.

And Trucker suddenly felt smaller than he ever had before.

At the top of the mountain,
Trucker pulled aside to rest.
He watched the mopeds zip around bends.
He gazed at the cars coasting along.
He smiled at the pick-ups tracing the ridges.

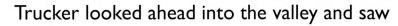

Trucker looked ahead into the valley and saw

Train's track reappear out of a tunnel.

"Oh no," Trucker whispered.

There!

Down below.

Train's tracks.

Another junction . . .

A broken-off gate!

"What if no one notices?" Trucker trembled.

"What if no one stops?"

Trucker hurtled down the mountain.

The mopeds swerved.

The cars pulled aside.

The pick-ups braked very, very hard.

Trucker's freight thrust down the mountain
with more speed than ever.

Errrrrrr!! Trucker stopped.

He turned.

He reversed.

He turned.

He reversed.

He HAD to block the road.

BEEP! BEEP! squeaked the mopeds.

Toot! Toot! piped the cars.

HONK! HONK! blared the pick-ups.

One by one, they came to a stop and stared Trucker down.

Trucker didn't like the beeps or the toots or the honks.

He wished the horns would stop.

He wished, this time, that Train could chug faster.

WOOOOOOOOOOOOOO! WOOOOOOOOOOOOOO!

Tic-a-tic-a clack. Tic-a-tic-a clack. Tic-a-tic-a clack.

Everything rattled. Trucker counted to himself —

2...4...6

Tic-a-tic-a clack.

Tic-a-tic-a clack.

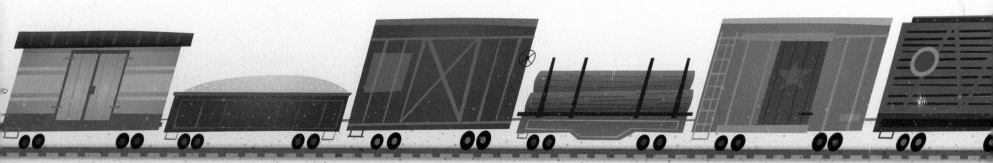

...8 ...10.

Tic-a-tic-a clack.

Tic-a-tic-a clack.

Train hurried off around the next bend
and out of everyone's sight.
And the valley fell silent.
Until . . .

WOOOOOOOOOO! WOOOOOOOOOO!

Off in the distance, Train let out a long, thankful whistle.

And one by one, the mopeds began to beep.

The cars began to cheer.

The pick-ups began to shimmy.

And Trucker started off, along with the others, happy to share the road.